ALICE NIZZY NAZZY

THE WITCH OF SANTA FE

by **Tony Johnston**

illustrated by **Tomie dePaola**

PAPERSTAR

The Putnam & Grosset Group

For Candace Lynch,
who said the magic words, "roadrunner-footed house,"
for the Horned Lizard Conservation Society,
and for Leon Gerson, whose Russian roots run deep.– T. J.

For Amanda, Thais, Christine and Davis Mather
who all know Santa Fe style!– T. deP. N. H.

Printed on recycled paper

Text copyright © 1995 by Tony Johnston
Illustrations copyright © 1995 by Tomie dePaola
A PaperStar Book, published in 1998 by The Putnam & Grosset Group, 200 Madison
Avenue, New York, NY 10016. PaperStar is a registered trademark of The Putnam
Berkley Group, Inc. The PaperStar logo is a trademark of The Putnam Berkley Group,
Inc. Originally published in 1995 by G. P. Putnam's Sons.
Published simultaneously in Canada. Printed in the United States of America.
Lettering by David Gatti. Book design by Patrick Collins. Text set in Aurelia.
Library of Congress Cataloging-in-Publication Data
Johnston, Tony. Alice Nizzy Nazzy, the Witch of Santa Fe / Tony Johnston;
illustrated by Tomie dePaola. p. cm.
Summary: When Manuela's sheep are stolen, she has to go to Alice Nizzy Nazzy's
talking road-runner-footed adobe house and try to get the witch to give the flock back.
[1. Witches—Fiction. 2. Southwest, New—Fiction.] I. DePaola, Tomie, ill. II. Title.
PZ7.J6478A1 1995 [E]—dc20 93-44375 CIP AC
ISBN 0-698-11650-X
10 9 8 7 6 5 4 3 2 1

Alice Nizzy Nazzy lived in the desert, near the *pueblo* of Santa Fe.
She was as old as rivers, as old as hills, as old as sandstone cliffs.
She was *so* old and *so* mean, people said she was a witch.

"Don't dare go near Alice Nizzy Nazzy," parents told their children.
"Or she will eat you up."

Alice Nizzy Nazzy's adobe hut stood on skinny roadrunner feet. Around it grew a fence of prickly pear. Whenever she mumbled certain words to the hut (or tickled its feet), the adobe carried her over the sizzling sand to find naughty children to eat. (And wherever the roadrunner-footed hut went, the cactus fence went too.)

One day a little girl named Manuela came by, looking for her lost sheep. Their tracks had led her straight up to the witch woman's fence. *Oh, my!*

When Manuela saw the strange adobe, she knew very well who lived there. (Who but Alice Nizzy Nazzy had a house with roadrunner feet?)

Manuela wanted to run away, but not without her sheep.
She peeked over the fence to see if they were there.
"Go away, you nosy child!" cried a prickly voice.
"What a beautiful talking fence!" Manuela breathed, though scared out of her wits.

The fence was so pleased, it opened itself up.
And she went in! *Oh, my!*
Manuela saw piles of skulls and bones in heaps.
But not a single sheep.

She peeked through a window of the roadrunner-footed
hut to see if they were there.

"Go away, you nosy child!" squawked a fowl voice.

"What a wonderful talking house!" Manuela breathed.

The adobe was so pleased, it opened its door.
And she went in! *Oh, my!*

She saw a cobweb hammock and dirty pillows everywhere.
But not a single sheep.
   She peeked into the kitchen to see if they were there.
   "Come in, you nosy child!" scraped a voice like gritty sand.
   And she went in! OH, MY!

There, sitting on a shelf, was——Alice Nizzy Nazzy herself!

Her face was withered as a walnut, and her skin was yellow as squash. Her eyes were red and beady and bright. Her teeth were black as night. (And they snapped like mousetraps.) Her hair was strings of chiles. Her belt was *conchos*, shiny as moons. And her velvet skirt swished like water when she moved.

Draped over her shoulder was a huge horned lizard.

"*Hola,*" the lizard said.

"What a lovely talking lizard!"

"*Gracias, dulce angelita.*"

"Shut your trap!" Alice Nizzy Nazzy snapped.

"She's no sweet angel. She's a naughty girl."

"I'm *good*," Manuela said. "I'm looking for my sheep. I followed them right here."

"Dear, dear, dear," croaked the crone, sly as can be. "No sheep here. Just some dirty old pillows. You *can't* be good. You lost a whole flock. I'll have to eat you up."

She cackled a cackle that could wear down cliffs and popped Manuela into the cooking pot. *Oh, my!*

The horned lizard groaned, *"Ay! Ay! Ay!"*

Though very frightened, Manuela looked around. In a corner she saw a cupboard with the face of a giant mask. "What's in there?" she asked.

"Ah," said Alice Nizzy Nazzy, adding chiles to the pot. "That's where I keep my special teas." Then she shouted, "Open up!"

WHOOOOOOOOOSH! The mask's great mouth flew open wide.
Shelves of jars were inside, stuffed to bursting with teas.
Teas for gashes. Teas for rashes. Teas for rickets. Teas for crickets.
Every jar was full of leaves–except one.

When the old woman saw that, her brow grew dark as a thunder-
head. "AY! AY! AY!" she cried.

"What's wrong?" asked Manuela from the cooking pot.

Alice Nizzy Nazzy wailed, "The empty jar. I forgot. It must be filled with petals from the black cactus flower. Only its tea will keep me young. I've searched every arroyo and rimrock and draw. It's nowhere to be found!"

Her voice rose high and higher.

Then she struck a match on her chin and lit the fire.

The lizard groaned, *"Ay! Ay! Ay!"*

Poor Manuela! All was lost!

Or was it?

Suddenly she shouted out, "I know where the black flower is!"

The wicked old woman's eyes got big as *sopaipillas*. Her mousetrap teeth champed. Her pointed feet stamped. The prickly pear fence tiptoed near to hear. The adobe stood stone still and listened.

"Where?" she asked, leaning close. (They were nearly nose to nose.)

The horned lizard whispered, *"No digas.* Don't tell."

"Hush, you bloated bag of scales!" Alice Nizzy Nazzy railed. Then she sweetly hissed, "Where's the black cactus flower? You can tell Auntie Alice."

"Only if you promise to give me my sheep."

"I promise." Alice Nizzy Nazzy smirked. (For it was a trick. She'd crossed her fingers behind her back.)

"*Ay! Ay! Ay!*" The lizard groaned when it saw that.

"It grows where my sheep graze," Manuela said. "I've seen it dozens of times."

"Where? Where? Where?"

"I'll take you there."

Alice Nizzy Nazzy yanked Manuela from the pot. They leaped
into a huge mortar and flew off, swirling like a storm.

Over mountains and mesas they soared.
Alice shrieked all the time, "Soon the black flower will be mine!"
Manuela pointed the way, up a canyon, steep and deep.

"There," she said at last, as they swooped to the top of a cliff.
Alice Nizzy Nazzy squinted her eyes, small and smaller. She saw
the prize. Growing on the very highest ledge was——the black
cactus flower!

The mortar landed with a THUMP. The witch jumped out, dashed right up to the cactus and ripped the magic flower off.

Instantly, thunder clapped and clashed. Lightning slashed the sky. And all weathers happened at once. OH, MY!

Then, cackling a cackle that could gouge out gorges, she steered them home again.

When they got there, Manuela said, "Now give me my flock."

Alice Nizzy Nazzy grinned and popped her back into the pot. (Oh, my! By then the water was getting hot!)

The lizard groaned, *"Ay! Ay! Ay!"*

Manuela cried, "But you promised."

"Sorry. My fingers were crossed."

Alice Nizzy Nazzy stirred her stew.

"Naughty children are so tasty," she said. (She threw *jicama* and *cilantro* in too.)

Noisily, she took a taste. She puckered her face and spit it out.

"You *are* a good child," she said with disgust. "Good children taste so *sour!*"

So Alice Nizzy Nazzy grabbed the magic flower, sprang into the mortar and steered herself away to find a naughty child.

"Hasta la vista." The horned lizard smiled. Manuela hopped out of the pot.

And the sheep?

The moment the old hag whirled off, her spell was broken. The dirty pillows became sheep again. They filled the adobe, baa-ing and bleating and bumping around.

That was too much for the roadrunner-footed hut. It bent over and dumped them all out.

And it ran off to find Alice Nizzy Nazzy. (The prickly pear fence ran right behind.)

Manuela was so glad to have her sheep, she hugged every single one. Then, with the horned lizard perched upon her head, she happily herded them home.

Author's Note

There's nothing like a good (bad) witch to stir the imagination. But the witch I love best, Russia's Baba Yaga, has a story told countless times. So, what do you do when your witch is taken? First you shout, "THUNDERATION!" Then you pack up her belongings–chicken-footed house, herbs, hexes–and move her to a snazzy new location. Give her a horned lizard for a pet, add some sheep (shades of Homer and Bo Peep), toss a shepherd girl into her cooking pot, and what have you got, anyway?–ALICE NIZZY NAZZY, THE WITCH OF SANTA FE.

–*T.J.*

Artist's Note

When Baba Yaga moved to Santa Fe, I was only too happy to accommodate her. I've traveled to Santa Fe many times, which made it easy for me to transform Baba Yaga's traditional surroundings of the wild woods of Russia into the dry desert of New Mexico. But, in case you were wondering, although Baba Yaga and Alice Nizzy Nazzy are close cousins, Alice bears no resemblance to dear Strega Nona. About the only thing *they* have in common is the unusual ability of each of their little houses to expand or shrink as the need arises.

–*T.deP. N.H.*